READING CORNER

PHONICS

Captain Rainbow

Practising long vowel phonemes,
trisyllabic words and tricky words

First published in 2007 by
Franklin Watts
338 Euston Road
London
NW1 3BH

Franklin Watts Australia
Level 17/207 Kent Street
Sydney
NSW 2000

Text © Sue Graves 2007
Illustration © Rory Walker 2007

A CIP catalogue record for this book is available
from the British Library.

ISBN: 978 0 7496 7285 0 (hbk)
ISBN: 978 0 7496 7323 9 (pbk)

Series Editor: Jackie Hamley
Series Advisors: Dr Barrie Wade, Dr Hilary Minns
Series Designer: Peter Scoulding

Printed in China

Franklin Watts is a division of
Hachette Children's Books.

PHONICS

Captain
Rainbow

by
Sue Graves

Illustrated by
Rory Walker

W
FRANKLIN WATTS
LONDON • SYDNEY

Sue Graves

"My children loved playing with toy boats in the bath. But they didn't have any that were as super as Captain Rainbow's."

Rory Walker

"I love the sea, so Captain Rainbow is very lucky to have such a nice boat. Maybe one day I will too!"

Captain Rainbow had a boat.

He had fun sailing it on the sea.

6

7

But there was a little hole
in the middle of the roof.

8

It began to rain.

The hole let in the rain.

Soon there was a big puddle.

Captain Rainbow had to put on his wellingtons!

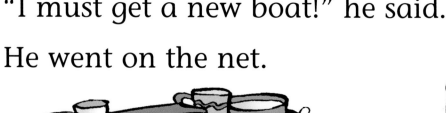

"I must get a new boat!" he said.

He went on the net.

He found the boat web page.

There was a
big boat ...

... and a
small boat.

There was a
power boot ...

... and a
sailing boat.

Then he saw just the boat.

It was red and green.

"I will get that boat!" he said.

Your boat will be sent on Friday.

A note came up on the web page.

"How lucky!" said Captain Rainbow. "I can sail my new boat at the weekend!"

On Friday, a big truck came.

"Parcel for Captain Rainbow!"
said the man.

23

"It can't be my boat," said Captain
Rainbow. "The parcel is too small.
And the bill is too small!"

In the parcel was a toy boat.

25

Captain Rainbow was sad. "How silly of me to get a toy boat," he said. "I can't sail on the sea in that!"

Then he began to smile.
"But," he said, "I know
where I *can* sail my boat!"

29

"Row, row, row your boat,
gently down the stream!"
he sang.

31

Notes for parents and teachers

READING CORNER PHONICS has been structured to provide maximum support for children learning to read through synthetic phonics. The stories are designed for independent reading but may also be used by adults for sharing with young children.

The teaching of early reading through synthetic phonics focuses on the 44 sounds in the English language, and how these sounds correspond to their written form in the 26 letters of the alphabet. Carefully controlled vocabulary makes these books accessible for children at different stages of phonics teaching, progressing from simple CVC (consonant-vowel-consonant) words such as "top" (t-o-p) to trisyllabic words such as "messenger" (mess-en-ger). READING CORNER PHONICS allows children to read words in context, and also provides visual clues and repetition to further support their reading. These books will help develop the all important confidence in the new reader, and encourage a love of reading that will last a lifetime!

If you are reading this book with a child, here are a few tips:

1. Talk about the story before you start reading. Look at the cover and the title. What might the story be about? Why might the child like it?

2. Encourage the child to reread the story, and to retell the story in their own words, using the illustrations to remind them what has happened.

3. Discuss the story and see if the child can relate it to their own experience, or perhaps compare it to another story they know.

4. Give praise! Small mistakes need not always be corrected. If a child is stuck on a word, ask them to try and sound it out and then blend it together again, or model this yourself. For example "wish" w-i-sh "wish".

READING CORNER PHONICS covers two grades of synthetic phonics teaching, with three levels at each grade. Each level has a certain number of words per story, indicated by the number of bars on the spine of the book:

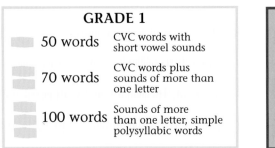

GRADE 1

50 words — CVC words with short vowel sounds

70 words — CVC words plus sounds of more than one letter

100 words — Sounds of more than one letter, simple polysyllabic words

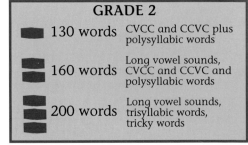

GRADE 2

130 words — CVCC and CCVC plus polysyllabic words

160 words — Long vowel sounds, CVCC and CCVC and polysyllabic words

200 words — Long vowel sounds, trisyllabic words, tricky words